Sir William Watson

The Eloping Angels

A Caprice

Sir William Watson

The Eloping Angels
A Caprice

ISBN/EAN: 9783744750035

Printed in Europe, USA, Canada, Australia, Japan

Cover: Foto ©Andreas Hilbeck / pixelio.de

More available books at **www.hansebooks.com**

ELOPING ANGELS

A CAPRICE

BY

WILLIAM WATSON

New York

MACMILLAN AND CO.

AND LONDON

1893

TO

GRANT ALLEN

AN ONLY TOO GENEROUS APPRECIATOR OF MY VERSE

I DEDICATE THIS POEM

KNOWING THAT HE WILL RECOGNISE

BENEATH ITS SOMEWHAT HAZARDOUS LEVITY

A SPIRIT NOT WHOLLY FLIPPANT

SUCH AS CAN ALONE JUSTIFY ITS INSCRIPTION

TO A SERIOUS LOVER OF THE MUSE

Written in September and October, 1892.

W. W.

FAUST, on a day, and Mephistopheles,

  In the dead season, were supremely bored.

'What shall we do, our jaded souls to please?'

  Said Faust to his Familiar and his lord.

'All pleasures have we tasted at our ease,

  All byeways of all sin have we explored.

What *shall* we do, our jaded souls to please?'

'Ah, what indeed?' said Mephistopheles.

A

To whom thus Faust: 'My Mephisto, thou art

   A devil of exceeding rich resource;

Hast in thy time played every human part,

   And braved the shafts of archangelic Force;

Thou carriest lightly in thy brain a chart

   Of all the worlds, and every planet's course:

Can'st not procure us, by thy wit's rare power,

Admission into heaven for half-an-hour?

'Thou know'st the approaches well; did'st learn to
  scale

The starriest heights, in thy distinguished Past:

The Seraphim as comrades thou could'st hail,

  And with Saint Peter an old friendship hast.

Some private influence surely would avail,

  Joined with the prestige of thy name and caste.

'Twould mightily amuse me, I declare,

For once to see how wags the world up there.'

Then Mephisto: 'You vastly underrate

  The hazards and the dangers, my good Sir

Peter is stony as his name; the gate,

  Excepting to invited guests, won't stir.

'Tis long since he and I were intimate:

  We differed; — but to bygones why refer?

However, there 's no want of windows; you

Could get a glimpse of heaven by peeping through.'

5

So, on the wings of magic power, these twain

   Ascended through the steep and giddy night;

And soon this earth and all it doth contain

   Shrank to a point of hesitating light,

Till, as they climbed those altitudes inane,

   The battlements celestial dawned in sight,

And domes and turrets made one golden gleam

Splendid beyond all splendour born of dream.

6

Unto a window in the heavenly wall,

  A casement open to the night, they came,

When Mephisto addressed his charge and thrall:

  'This sort of prank, to me, is rather tame,

And my concern with Paradise is small:

  My int'rests lie elsewhere; but all the same,

You, as a stranger, might do worse than cast

A glance inside: most probably, your last.'

'Soft!' answered Faust, 'I hear a voice within,

   And if it be not some enamoured youth

Breathing warm words a maiden's heart to win,

   Like any mortal wooer, in good sooth

Thou 'rt not the great artificer of sin,

   Nor I a seeker after hidden truth.

Nay, sure enough — look! — what a charming pair!

Such eyes she has! And that auroral hair!'

Faust had not erred. These angels were indeed

  Two human lovers, who, by sudden fate,

Full early from the yoke of life being freed,

  Renewed their vows in that celestial state.

Now Faust, although immoral, was, I need

  Hardly affirm, a gentleman. 'I hate,'

He said, 'to play the spy at scenes like this.'

So he coughed loudly on their whispering bliss.

'Immortal Spirits! Beatitudes divine!

Behold,' he said, 'two wanderers from that star

Whence haply ye too hail: whose glories shine

Lost in deep space, so faint and pale they are.

If ye will graciously an ear incline,

And parley with us travellers from afar,

Fain would we learn such news as may be given

Of what — in short — is going on in heaven.'

B

'Friends, for such tidings ye in vain apply

To me,' the radiant Youth Angelic said.

'We lead a life withdrawn, this maid and I,

Nor love the life by other angels led —

All idle hymns of praise to the Most High.

Our one supreme desire is to be wed,

And we were even now concerting schemes

How to escape and realise our dreams.

II

'For here in heaven no marrying is, nor yet

    Giving in marriage, and we dwell debarred

From that full tie whereon our hearts are set —

    An inhibition surely somewhat hard.

One only hindrance — a most serious let —

    Doth still the moment of our flight retard:

To wit, this garb angelic, which on earth

Would comment cause, and haply move to mirth.'

'No bar at all!' quoth Mephisto the shrewd.

'You shall change wardrobes with my friend and
me.

Our earthly vesture when you have endued, —

'Tis somewhat picturesque, as you may see, —

Across the interstellar solitude

Safely to earth (dear planet!) you shall flee.

You have my blessing, both of you.   And now

We will effect the exchange, if you 'll allow.'

Merely to will, when spirit with spirit deals,

    Is to perform. The bargain once being made,

Faust, in a thought, appears from head to heels

    Clad in the garments of the angel-maid,

She in his own; the devil quite pious feels,

    In garb of heaven becomingly arrayed;

While the Bright Lover clothes divine desire

In most unhallowed and unblest attire.

So Faust and his companion entered, by

  The window, the abodes where seraphs dwell.

'Already morning quickens in the sky,

  And soon will sound the heavenly matin-bell;

Our time is short,' said Mephisto, 'for I

  Have an appointment about noon in hell.

Dear, dear! why, heaven has hardly changed one bit

Since the old days before the historic split.'

But leave we now this enterprising pair,

    Faust the explorer, Mephisto the guide,

And follow yon bright fugitives in their

    Ethereal journey whither mortals bide.

Across the wastes of space and fields of air

    Tireless they sped, and soon this orb descried,

Hung like a fairy lamp with timid gleam

    From the great branches of the Solar Scheme.

She, on the earth, a village girl, and he

  A prince had been. 'Twas pure romance of love,

Idyllic and ideal as could be,

  All policy and prudence far above.

And when he fell in glorious battle, she

  Could not survive him, poor, white, mateless dove!

And now on earth they stepped once more, and met

The ghosts of old dead kisses deathless yet.

'Twas morn. The lark was making for the sky,

  The ploughman was returning to his plough.

' Unto my father's palace we will fly,'

  Said the angelic Prince. 'Another, now,

Sits on his throne, but loyally will I

  Serve him, and gladly to his sceptre bow ;

And us, I doubt not, he will entertain,

And cheerly bid us welcome home again.'

So, to the royal palace having flown,

　And in no form or due observance failed,

With mien of homage they approached the throne;

　But the poor craven king in terror quailed,

Shrieking: 'More spectres! Out, ye sprites, begone!

　Have all my exorcists not yet availed

To rid me of these ghostly plagues that make

Life dreadful, if I sleep or if I wake?'

Then, with sad eyes compassionate, the twain

   Faded from out the presence, nothing loth

The presence of the fields and skies to gain.

   And she, the queen of his rich love and troth,

Spake very softly: 'Dearest, wilt thou deign

   To seek my father's cottage, where for both

Shall room and welcome be? for he doth own

A heart more royal than thy kinsman's throne.'

20

Unto her father's cot they took their way.

They found him leaning on his gate, white-haired,

Full of the memory of a former day.

Calmly he greeted them, like one prepared

For loftiest visitants, as who should say:

'My son and daughter, that so far have fared,

I have awaited you this many a year.

Enter and rest, my son and daughter dear.'

And entering in, they veiled their heavenly sheen

    In homely vesture, and themselves resigned

To homely tasks. A milkmaid or a queen,

    Her had you deemed: an emperor him, or hind.

Of port majestic, yet of humblest mien —

    Immortals, thrilled with touch of mortal kind —

To notes of earth they gave a sphery tone,

And knit the hearts of all things with their own.

So there they stayed, and to the neighbours few

 The story of their earthward flight revealed;

And more than paradisal bliss they drew

 From the familiar life of hearth and field.

Content with pleasures which the lowliest knew,

 The wealth which all things unto all things yield,

They vowed that nought should ever them decoy

Back to their selfish heaven of unearned joy.

23

Yet theirs were many griefs, for evermore

    They made the pangs of other hearts their own,

Feeling all pain they saw; and thus they bore

    The burden of the universal moan,

Wept with all tears, and with all wounds were sore.

    But likewise all the joy by others known

Became their joy; and in the world-wide scale,

Pleasure, they found, o'er pain did still prevail.

So, on the earth, as angels they remained,

Yet more than angels, being lovers too;

All their celestial loveliness retained,

And evermore in earthly sweetness grew.

Thus lost they nothing of divine, and gained

Everything human save what men must rue,

Uniting all below with all above,

Linking the stars and flowers in perfect love.

25

But being deathless, ever 'twas their doom,

   Loving their fellows, to lament them dead.

Age after age, they saw the opening tomb,

   And saw it close upon a comrade's head.

Yet what the grave took from them, that the womb

   Gave back; 'for death is but a form,' they said,

' Birth a convention : nought is less or more;

And nature but reclaimeth to restore.'

D

And still they tarry. I have met them oft,

  With their pure voices and caressing eyes.

You hear the rustle of their raiment soft,

  And looking up, behold with no surprise

The coronal they never yet have doffed,

  The lucid aureole worn in Paradise:

Nor can you marvel that they never cared

For joys which only idle angels shared.

*   *   *   *   *

27

'I think,' said Faust — himself and Mephisto

    Had just returned from their ethereal jaunt —

'This earth is still the nicest place I know.

    It always teases me when people flaunt

Their own superior bliss before me, so

    Aggressively, as in that sinless haunt

Where we have just been privileged to see

The dullness of entire felicity.

'And then, their bliss itself — no objects new

Tempting the soul for ever forth to press!

One goal attained, another half in view,

One riddle solved, another still to guess,

Something subdued and something to subdue,

Are the conditions of our happiness.

I know no harsher ordinance of fate

Than the stagnation of your perfect state.'

29

'All which,' said Mephisto, ' I've heard before.

Well, you and I no risk need apprehend

Of being stranded on that tedious shore.

From all such perils we are safe, my friend,

So make yourself quite easy on that score,

And your great mind to other matters bend.

Meanwhile, old fellow, Earth for you and me!

(*Aside.*) How he will take to *my* place, we shall see.'